Candy Cane Conjurations

Candy Cane Conjurations

Matthew Petchinsky

Candy Cane Conjurations
By: Matthew Petchinsky

Introduction: The Sweet Magic of Christmas

The holidays bring with them an unmistakable magic—a unique blend of warmth, wonder, and the promise of miracles. Among the shimmering lights, snow-dusted rooftops, and heartwarming traditions, one symbol has remained quietly powerful, carrying an ancient magic often overlooked: the humble candy cane.

To many, candy canes are simply festive treats, a cheerful splash of red and white nestled in stockings or dangling from Christmas trees. But look closer, and you'll find they are so much more. These sugary delights are not mere confections but potent conduits of ancient Christmas magic, imbued with the power to protect joy, spread love, and even conjure miracles.

The origins of this magical tradition trace back to the time of the **Holiday Magicians**, an elusive order of enchanted individuals dedicated to preserving the spirit of Christmas. In a world teetering between celebration and despair, these magicians understood the importance of safeguarding the intangible but vital essence of the season—an essence they called **Yuletide Glow**. They believed this glow was not just the heart of Christmas but the force that united families, inspired generosity, and filled hearts with hope.

To ensure the Yuletide Glow could withstand threats from darkness and doubt, the Holiday Magicians crafted candy canes as their ultimate talismans. They chose a simple design to hide extraordinary power. The red and white stripes represent the dual forces that sustain the season: love and purity. The crook at the top is not just a playful shape but a symbol of the shepherd's staff, a reminder to gather and guide loved ones, and of Christmas's protective magic. The sweet peppermint flavor is said to hold restorative energy, capable of soothing weary souls and rekindling holiday cheer.

Enchanted candy canes were scattered across the world, placed where they could weave their magic quietly, mending fractured families, softening hardened hearts, and turning even the coldest winter nights into celebrations of warmth and wonder. Legends whisper of candy canes that sparked impossible reunions, granted secret wishes, and shielded homes from the dark forces that prey on broken spirits during the holiday season.

Over time, the magic of candy canes has woven itself so seamlessly into Christmas traditions that many have forgotten its true origin. Yet, their magic remains. Every candy cane you hold carries a spark of that original enchantment, a legacy from the Holiday Magicians who knew that even the smallest gestures of sweetness and love could create ripples of magic throughout the world.

This book invites you to rediscover the sweet magic of Christmas, starting with the story of the candy cane. As you read, you'll uncover tales of their origins, learn how to wield their protective power, and explore the whimsical adventures they've inspired. Let this journey remind you that even in the simplest holiday traditions lies a profound and enduring magic, ready to protect, heal, and inspire.

So, unwrap a candy cane. Hold it close. You might just feel the Yuletide Glow stirring within you, ready to rekindle the magic of Christmas once more.

Chapter 1: The Secret of the Peppermint Grove

Mia never thought her Christmas holiday would be anything more than the usual blend of cozy sweaters, twinkling lights, and endless cups of cocoa. At 12 years old, she had grown accustomed to the same routines year after year: decorating the tree, watching classic holiday movies, and helping her grandmother, Nan, prepare for their family Christmas dinner. It was comforting, predictable, and perhaps a little dull. But this year, everything was about to change.

It all began on a snowy December afternoon as Mia rummaged through her grandmother's attic, searching for ornaments to decorate the tree. The scent of cinnamon and pine filled the air, and the attic was a treasure trove of memories, brimming with dusty boxes, forgotten keepsakes, and strings of tangled lights. As Mia reached for an old, wooden chest labeled *Holiday Delights,* something peculiar happened. A faint, sweet scent of peppermint wafted through the air, and the chest seemed to hum beneath her fingers.

"Nan!" Mia called, her voice echoing through the attic. "What's in this chest? It smells like candy!"

Her grandmother appeared moments later, her silver hair tucked under a knitted cap and her cheeks rosy from the cold. A mysterious smile played on her lips as she approached the chest.

"Oh, Mia," Nan said, her voice tinged with nostalgia. "You've found it. I was wondering when the chest would call to you."

"Call to me?" Mia asked, her brow furrowed in confusion. "It's just a box of ornaments, isn't it?"

Nan knelt beside the chest and placed a hand gently on its lid. "No, my dear. This chest is the key to a secret I've kept for many years—a secret that you are now old enough to learn."

With a flourish, Nan opened the chest, revealing not ornaments but a collection of candy canes. They were unlike any Mia had ever seen. Their red and white stripes shimmered as if made from liquid light, and the scent of peppermint grew so strong that Mia felt an instant wave of comfort and happiness.

"These are no ordinary candy canes," Nan said, her tone growing serious. "They come from the Peppermint Grove—a magical place hidden deep within the woods behind our house."

Mia's eyes widened. "The woods? You mean the place you always told me not to go?"

"Yes," Nan admitted. "I told you that to protect the grove. But now, I need your help. The grove is in danger, and without its magic, Christmas joy will begin to fade across the world."

Intrigued and more than a little skeptical, Mia pressed her grandmother for answers. Nan explained that she was once a **holiday conjurer**, a guardian of Christmas magic who worked alongside others to ensure the season's enchantment remained strong. The candy canes of the Peppermint Grove were the most potent magical artifacts under their care. Enchanted by the **Holiday Magicians** centuries ago, the candy canes infused the world with joy, generosity, and wonder. But now, their magic was waning.

"The grove's magic is tied to the purity of the Yuletide Glow," Nan continued. "For years, the glow has been dimming as people forget the true spirit of Christmas. Without someone to restore it, the candy canes will lose their power, and the world will grow colder, less kind, and more selfish with each passing year."

Mia felt a strange mixture of awe and disbelief. "So... you want me to help? What can I do? I'm just a kid."

Nan took her hands, her eyes twinkling with a mix of hope and determination. "You're more than you realize, Mia. The grove has chosen you. Its magic called to you because you have the courage and heart needed for the task ahead."

Nan explained that to restore the grove's magic, Mia would need to undertake a quest. It wasn't going to be easy. The grove's enchantment had been weakened by forces of doubt, greed, and despair—negative energies that had taken physical form as shadowy beings called **Frostlings.**

These creatures thrived in the absence of joy and were determined to snuff out the Yuletide Glow entirely.

To succeed, Mia would have to journey to the heart of the Peppermint Grove, locate the **Crystalline Cane of Origin,** and rekindle its light by performing a forgotten ritual. Along the way, she would face trials that tested her bravery, kindness, and belief in the magic of Christmas.

"But I can't do this alone," Mia said, her voice trembling slightly. "What if I fail?"

"You won't be alone," Nan reassured her. "I'll guide you as best as I can. And remember, the magic of the candy canes will help you. Each one carries a spark of the original enchantment, and if used wisely, they can protect you from harm."

Mia looked at the shimmering candy canes in the chest, their glow casting soft, colorful reflections on the attic walls. Something deep inside her stirred—a sense of purpose she hadn't felt before. She didn't know how, but she felt certain that she could do this. Christmas was counting on her.

"I'll do it," Mia said, her voice steady. "I'll save the grove."

Nan smiled, her expression both proud and a little sad. "Good. Then there's no time to waste. The Frostlings are growing stronger, and the grove needs you now more than ever."

As Mia prepared to embark on her journey, she couldn't shake the feeling that her life was about to change forever. What began as an ordinary holiday had turned into the adventure of a lifetime—an adventure that would reveal the true magic of Christmas and the strength she never knew she had.

And so, with a shimmering candy cane in hand and her grandmother's words of encouragement echoing in her ears, Mia took her first step toward the Peppermint Grove, ready to uncover its secrets and fight for the magic of Christmas.

Chapter 2: The Recipe for Renewal

The next morning, Mia awoke to the sound of soft chimes and the faint scent of peppermint lingering in the air. For a moment, she thought it had all been a dream—the candy canes, her grandmother's revelations, the looming threat to Christmas magic. But when she sat up in bed, she saw a peculiar book on her nightstand, its cover shimmering like frost under moonlight.

The book was old but pristine, its leather binding embossed with swirling candy cane patterns. Across the top, in ornate golden script, it read:

"The Yuletide Codex: Recipes for Renewal."

Mia's fingers trembled as she opened it. The pages glowed faintly, and the letters shifted and danced as if alive. Just as she began to read, Nan entered the room, carrying a tray with hot cocoa and a plate of sugar cookies.

"I see the Codex found you," Nan said with a warm smile.

"It's incredible," Mia whispered, her eyes scanning the first page, which described the importance of re-enchanting the candy canes to restore the Yuletide Glow. "But this looks... complicated."

Nan set the tray down and sat beside her. "It's no small task, Mia. The recipe for re-enchantment requires rare ingredients from places most people only read about in fairy tales. But with determination—and a little help—you can do it."

As if on cue, a faint tapping sound came from the window. Mia turned to see a candy cane perched on the sill, balancing on its crook like a bird. It hopped inside with surprising agility and landed on her desk.

"Hello there!" the candy cane said, its voice cheerful and slightly nasal. Its stripes shimmered as it spoke, and its round tip bobbed in greeting. "Name's Cane. I'll be your guide on this little adventure of ours."

Mia stared, her mouth agape. "A talking candy cane?"

Cane puffed up with pride. "Not just any candy cane. I'm the last of the original enchanted batch, and I've got all the know-how you'll need to complete this mission. Think of me as your magical GPS—only way cooler."

Nan chuckled. "Cane has been with our family for generations. He'll be an invaluable ally on your journey."

Still trying to wrap her head around the situation, Mia turned back to the Codex. On the first page of the recipe for renewal, a list of ingredients glowed softly:

- **Stardust Sugar**: Harvested from the glowing sands of the Celestial Confectionery, a floating island in the night sky.
- **Frozen Mint Crystals**: Guarded by the Ice Elves in the Frosted Vale.
- **Aurora Honey**: Collected from the hives of the Northern Lights Bees.
- **Gingerroot Essence**: Found in the labyrinthine caves of the Gingerbread Mountains.
- **Cinnamon Spark**: The fiery spice mined from the heart of the Ember Pines.

As Mia read, a deep sense of dread settled in her stomach. These weren't just rare ingredients—they were nearly impossible to obtain.

"How am I supposed to get all of this?" she asked. "The Celestial Confectionery? The Ice Elves? These places sound... dangerous."

"They can be," Nan admitted, "but you won't be alone. Cane knows the way, and you'll have help from a friend." She turned to the door, where a shaggy-haired boy peeked in, his grin wide and mischievous.

"Morning, Mia!" Toby said, stepping into the room. "Heard you're going on a quest to save Christmas. Mind if I tag along?"

"Toby?" Mia asked, raising an eyebrow. "How do you even know about this?"

"I may have overheard a certain peppermint stick talking to your Nan last night," Toby admitted, shrugging. "Come on, you'll need someone to watch your back—and who better than me?"

Mia opened her mouth to protest, but Nan cut in. "He's right, Mia. Every hero needs companions. And trust me, Toby will be more helpful than you think."

Mia sighed. "Fine. But don't slow me down."

"Slow you down? I'll be the one pulling you out of trouble!" Toby teased, grabbing one of the sugar cookies.

Cane cleared his throat—or at least made a sound resembling one. "Now that introductions are out of the way, we've got work to do. The first ingredient on our list is **Stardust Sugar.** We'll need to travel to the Celestial Confectionery, a floating island in the night sky. It's only accessible by a special candy cane portal, and guess what? I happen to know where one is."

"Let me guess," Mia said, her skepticism returning. "In the woods?"

"Bingo!" Cane said, spinning on his tip. "The Peppermint Grove has a hidden portal. But fair warning: the Frostlings are already lurking. They'll do whatever they can to stop us."

"Then we'd better be prepared," Mia said, her resolve hardening. She flipped through the Codex until she found a page titled **Basic Confectionery Charms.** It described how to use enchanted candy canes for protection, light, and even temporary invisibility.

Nan handed her a pouch filled with shimmering candy canes. "These are for emergencies. Use them wisely."

"Thanks, Nan," Mia said, hugging her grandmother tightly.

With Cane perched on her shoulder like a tiny, striped parrot and Toby armed with a sturdy walking stick, Mia set off for the Peppermint Grove. The weight of the Codex in her satchel reminded her of the daunting task ahead, but for the first time, she felt a flicker of hope.

As they trudged through the snow, Cane began explaining the dangers of their first destination. The Celestial Confectionery was a wondrous place, but it was protected by sentient sugar clouds that could trap intruders in sticky storms. To harvest the Stardust Sugar, they would need to locate the **Sands of Radiance**, a glowing dune hidden within the island's labyrinth of sweets.

"Piece of cake," Toby said, grinning.

"More like a slice of *impossible,*" Cane muttered.

The journey had begun, and though the path ahead was uncertain, Mia knew one thing for sure: saving Christmas would require every ounce of courage, wit, and magic she could muster.

Chapter 3: Trials of the Frosted Forest

The Frosted Forest loomed ahead, its towering sugar-glazed trees sparkling like crystalline sculptures under the pale winter sun. The air was crisp and sweet, tinged with the faint scent of vanilla, but an eerie silence hung over the forest. Snow blanketed the ground in a glittering sheet, untouched by tracks or signs of life. Mia tightened her grip on her satchel, the Codex tucked safely inside. Toby walked beside her, twirling his walking stick, while Cane perched on her shoulder, humming an off-key version of "Jingle Bells."

"This place gives me the creeps," Toby muttered, his breath puffing into the chilly air. "It's too... quiet."

"That's the point," Cane said, his voice unusually serious. "The Frosted Forest is enchanted to keep intruders out. It's not just quiet—it's listening. So, keep your wits about you."

As they ventured deeper into the forest, the temperature seemed to drop, and the path became increasingly narrow, flanked by trees whose branches formed an archway of frosted candy. The shimmering beauty of the place was undeniable, but Mia couldn't shake the feeling that they were being watched.

Suddenly, a soft, tinkling laugh echoed through the trees. Then another, and another, until it sounded like a chorus of wind chimes. Mia and Toby stopped in their tracks, exchanging nervous glances.

"What was that?" Mia whispered.

"Sugar Sprites," Cane said, his voice low. "Tricksters, but harmless... mostly. They guard the Stardust Sugar and won't let anyone pass without solving their riddles. Be careful—if you answer wrong, the forest has a way of... dealing with it."

Before Mia could respond, the air shimmered, and tiny figures materialized in front of them. The Sugar Sprites were no larger than teacups, their translucent wings sparkling like spun sugar. Each Sprite glowed faintly in hues of pastel pink, blue, or green, their eyes twinkling with mischief.

"Well, well, well," one of the Sprites said, her voice as sweet as honey but laced with a sharp edge. "Visitors in the Frosted Forest? How delightful!"

Another Sprite, this one glowing a bright minty green, flew closer. "What brings you to our domain? Seeking the Stardust Sugar, perhaps?"

"Yes," Mia said, her voice steady despite the butterflies in her stomach. "We need it to restore the magic of Christmas."

The Sprites exchanged amused glances, their laughter chiming like bells. The green Sprite spoke again. "If you wish to take the Stardust Sugar, you must prove your worth. The rules are simple: solve our riddles, and we will grant you passage. Fail, and the forest will claim you."

"Claim us?" Toby asked, taking a step back. "What does that mean?"

"Let's not find out," Cane interjected, nudging Mia forward. "Go on, kid. You've got this."

The first Sprite hovered in front of Mia, her wings beating rapidly. "Here is your first riddle:

I am not alive, but I grow;
I don't have lungs, but I need air;
I don't have a mouth, and yet I drown. What am I?"

Mia frowned, her mind racing. She could feel the weight of the Sprite's gaze, sharp and unyielding. "Not alive, but it grows... no lungs, but it needs air..." Then it clicked.

"Fire," Mia said confidently.

The Sprite clapped her hands, a shower of sparkling sugar falling from her wings. "Correct! But don't celebrate yet. There are more to come."

Another Sprite stepped forward, her glow a pale lavender. "My turn! Here is my riddle:

The more of me you take, the more you leave behind. What am I?"

Toby scratched his head, muttering under his breath. "The more you take, the more you leave behind... footsteps! It's footsteps!"

The Sprite nodded approvingly. "Very good. Perhaps you're cleverer than you look."

"Thanks, I think?" Toby muttered, but Cane nudged him with a chuckle.

The final Sprite, her glow a bright orange, floated forward. Her expression was more serious than the others. "Your final challenge:

I have cities, but no houses; forests, but no trees; rivers, but no water. What am I?"

This one stumped Mia. She closed her eyes, replaying the riddle in her head. "Cities but no houses... forests but no trees... rivers but no water..." Her gaze dropped to the Codex, and suddenly, the answer came to her.

"A map," she said, her voice steady.

The Sprite's face broke into a grin. "Correct! You have proven your cleverness, but that is not enough to pass."

"What do you mean?" Mia asked, her heart sinking.

The Sprite's expression darkened. "The forest is under threat. A creature of bitterness, the Sourling, lurks in the shadows, feeding on lost holiday cheer. It seeks to destroy the magic of this place. To retrieve the Stardust Sugar, you must face it."

As if on cue, a low growl echoed through the trees, sending shivers down Mia's spine. The Sprites disappeared in a flash of light, leaving the companions alone.

"Why do they always leave when it gets dangerous?" Toby muttered, gripping his walking stick.

The growling grew louder, and the air turned heavy, filled with the acrid scent of sour lemons. From the shadows emerged the Sourling, a grotesque creature with twisted limbs and a mouth that dripped with acidic saliva. Its eyes glowed with malevolence, and its very presence seemed to sap the joy from the air.

Cane leaped from Mia's shoulder. "Stay close to me! The Sourling feeds on fear and despair. You have to resist it!"

The Sourling lunged, but Mia held her ground, pulling a candy cane from her pouch. Remembering the Codex's instructions, she whispered a charm under her breath. The candy cane glowed, forming a shield of light that deflected the creature's attack.

Toby, showing surprising bravery, swung his walking stick, knocking the Sourling back. "Take that, you sour freak!"

"Nice swing!" Cane cheered. "But we need to end this!"

Mia focused, her heart pounding. Drawing another candy cane, she recited a second charm. This time, the candy cane transformed into a glowing whip of peppermint light. With a crack, she lashed at the Sourling, driving it back into the shadows. The forest seemed to exhale as the creature retreated, its bitter presence fading.

The Sprites reappeared, their expressions a mix of awe and gratitude. "You have done what we could not," the green Sprite said. "You have driven the Sourling away, at least for now. The Stardust Sugar is yours."

A path of glowing light appeared before them, leading to a clearing where the Stardust Sugar shimmered in a crystalline heap. Mia carefully collected a handful, placing it in a glass vial Nan had given her.

"Thank you," she said to the Sprites.

The green Sprite nodded. "Thank you, brave travelers. But beware—the Sourling will return, and your journey is far from over."

As they left the Frosted Forest, Mia couldn't help but feel a mix of pride and trepidation. One challenge was behind them, but many more lay ahead. For the first time, though, she felt the stirrings of true confidence. With her companions by her side, she was ready to face whatever came next.

Chapter 4: The Battle for Sweetness

The Frosted Vale stretched before them, a glittering expanse of icy peaks and snow-laden valleys. Frosted trees shimmered like diamonds, their branches coated in a thick layer of crystalline frost. The air was frigid, biting at Mia's cheeks as she trudged forward, her breath forming wispy clouds. The Codex's instructions had led them to this desolate yet beautiful place, the final destination on their journey to collect the Frozen Mint Crystals. But as beautiful as it was, the Vale held an ominous stillness that set Mia on edge.

Toby's footsteps crunched in the snow behind her, and Cane perched on her shoulder, glowing faintly as if to offer warmth.

"Frozen Mint Crystals," Cane said, his tone unusually serious, "aren't just rare—they're fiercely protected by the Ice Elves. They don't take kindly to strangers poking around in their territory. We'll need to be careful."

"Great," Toby muttered, tightening his grip on his walking stick. "Just what we needed—more riddles and traps."

"It's not just the Elves I'm worried about," Mia said, scanning the frozen expanse. "The Sourling is still out there. If it catches us here, we might not have a way out."

The three pushed forward, following the Codex's directions to a cave hidden within the Vale's tallest peak. Inside, the walls sparkled with frost, and a faint, minty aroma filled the air. In the center of the cavern was a pedestal made of pure ice, atop which the Frozen Mint Crystals glowed softly, their radiance illuminating the space.

"We found it!" Toby exclaimed, stepping toward the pedestal.

"Wait!" Cane shouted. "The Ice Elves—"

Before Cane could finish, a sharp whistle cut through the air, and from the shadows emerged a group of figures. The Ice Elves were tall and slender, their skin pale blue and their eyes like shards of ice. They moved with eerie grace, their spears glinting in the crystalline light.

"Thieves," one of the Elves hissed, their voice cold and commanding. "You dare trespass in our sacred cavern?"

"We're not here to steal," Mia said quickly, stepping forward with her hands raised. "We need the Frozen Mint Crystals to save Christmas. The magic of the candy canes is fading, and without it, the spirit of the season will be lost."

The Elves exchanged wary glances, their expressions unreadable. Finally, the leader spoke. "The crystals are not yours to take. Prove your intentions are pure, or you will leave empty-handed."

Mia opened the Codex, scanning the pages for guidance. A passage about the Ice Elves caught her eye: *They are creatures of honor and will test the heart of any who seek their treasures.*

"I'm ready," she said, her voice steady.

The leader nodded and stepped aside, revealing a large, ice-carved mirror behind them. "Step forward and face the Reflection of Truth."

Mia hesitated, her heart pounding. The mirror's surface swirled like liquid ice, and as she approached, her reflection began to shift. Instead of seeing herself, she saw images of her past—times when she had been selfish or afraid, when she had doubted her own strength. The images stung, but she refused to look away.

Then the mirror changed, showing her recent journey: solving the Sprites' riddles, standing her ground against the Sourling, protecting Toby, and trusting Cane. These moments filled her with warmth, a reminder of how far she had come.

The mirror's surface stilled, and the Elves lowered their spears. The leader stepped forward, their expression softening. "Your heart is true, and your purpose noble. The crystals are yours."

Mia carefully collected the Frozen Mint Crystals, placing them in a small velvet pouch. But as she turned to thank the Elves, a deep, guttural growl echoed through the cavern, freezing everyone in place.

The Sourling had found them.

Its grotesque form slithered from the shadows, its eyes glowing with malice. The cavern's temperature plummeted as its bitter aura filled the space, snuffing out the warmth of the crystals.

"You cannot stop me," the Sourling hissed, its voice dripping with venom. "The bitterness of the world is too strong. The magic of Christmas will fall, and all will know despair."

The Ice Elves stepped back, their faces pale with fear. Cane jumped from Mia's shoulder, glowing brightly. "Mia! Use the crystals! Their magic can counteract its bitterness!"

Mia reached for the pouch, but the Sourling lunged, swiping at her with clawed hands. Toby stepped in, swinging his stick with surprising force, driving the creature back.

"Hurry up, Mia!" Toby shouted.

Mia pulled a candy cane from her satchel and whispered a conjuration she had learned from the Codex. The candy cane glowed, its light combining with the radiant energy of the Frozen Mint Crystals. A warm, minty breeze filled the cavern, pushing back the Sourling's darkness.

The creature screeched, its form twisting as the light enveloped it. "You cannot destroy me!" it cried. "Bitterness cannot be erased!"

"No," Mia said, her voice firm. "But it can be transformed."

She closed her eyes, focusing on the Sourling's essence. Bitterness was born from pain, she realized—from lost joy and forgotten hope. If she could remind it of sweetness, it might change.

Mia channeled the magic of the candy canes, their essence infused with love, joy, and the spirit of the season. The light grew brighter, wrapping around the Sourling like a warm embrace. Its twisted form began to shift, shrinking and softening until it was no longer a creature of darkness but a small, glowing figure—a joyful spirit with bright eyes and a warm smile.

The Ice Elves watched in awe as the transformed Sourling floated toward Mia. "Thank you," it said, its voice now soft and melodic. "You have reminded me of what I once was."

The spirit floated upward, merging with the Frozen Mint Crystals. The cavern glowed brighter than ever, the magic of the crystals restored.

The Ice Elves bowed deeply. "You have done what we could not," their leader said. "You have saved the crystals and the spirit of the Vale. Go, and may your journey bring light to the world."

As Mia, Toby, and Cane left the cavern, the warmth of their success filled them with hope. The final ingredient was theirs, and the power of the candy canes was one step closer to being restored. But more importantly, Mia had learned that even the darkest bitterness could be turned sweet with a little magic and a lot of heart.

Chapter 5: The Great Confection Conjuration

The return to the Peppermint Grove was both triumphant and bittersweet. Mia, Toby, and Cane had overcome impossible odds, traveling through enchanted realms, solving riddles, and facing down the Sourling. Each of the rare ingredients they carried felt like a trophy, but the weight of their mission still pressed heavily on Mia's heart. If the re-enchantment ceremony failed, all their efforts would have been for nothing—and Christmas magic would fade forever.

The grove was alive with an ethereal glow when they arrived. The towering peppermint trees hummed faintly, their candy-striped trunks radiating warmth. Snow glittered like powdered sugar under the starlit sky, and the air was filled with the familiar scent of peppermint, sweeter and richer than Mia had ever remembered.

Nan was waiting for them in the heart of the grove, standing before a stone altar carved with intricate candy cane patterns. She wore a cloak embroidered with shimmering silver threads, her presence regal and reassuring. Around her, the grove seemed to pulse with anticipation, as though the very magic of the land awaited their next move.

"You've done well, Mia," Nan said, her voice warm but tinged with gravity. "But the hardest part lies ahead. The re-enchantment ceremony is no simple spell. It requires precision, focus, and, above all, belief."

Mia swallowed hard, stepping forward to place her satchel on the altar. The Codex glowed faintly as she opened it, turning to the page that detailed the **Great Confection Conjuration.** The instructions were written in curling golden script, the words shimmering with enchantment:

Combine the ingredients of joy and sweetness to rekindle the Yuletide Glow. Speak the incantation with an open heart, and the magic will awaken once more.

Nan motioned for Mia to lay out the ingredients. With careful hands, Mia placed the **Stardust Sugar**, its grains glowing like tiny stars, next to the **Frozen Mint Crystals**, which radiated an icy blue light.

The **Aurora Honey** glimmered with iridescent hues, and the **Gingerroot Essence** exuded a warm, spicy aroma. Finally, the **Cinnamon Spark** flickered like embers, casting shadows that danced across the snow.

"Each of these ingredients carries a piece of the season's magic," Nan explained. "Together, they form the foundation of the candy canes' enchantment. But it is your heart, Mia, that will breathe life into them."

Mia nodded, her pulse quickening. "What do I have to do?"

"You must combine the ingredients using the ceremonial candy cane," Nan said, producing a large, ornate candy cane from her cloak. Its stripes shimmered with every color of the rainbow, and its crook was adorned with tiny bells that chimed softly. "And then, you must speak the incantation written in the Codex."

Cane hopped onto the altar, his usual playfulness replaced by solemnity. "No pressure, kid, but this is kind of a one-shot deal. If you mess up, the ingredients will lose their potency."

"Thanks for the pep talk," Mia said dryly, earning a chuckle from Toby.

Taking a deep breath, Mia picked up the ceremonial candy cane. Its weight felt significant, as though it carried the hopes of every child who had ever believed in the magic of Christmas. She began mixing the ingredients on the altar, using the candy cane to stir them into a swirling, luminescent paste. The air around her seemed to vibrate with energy, and the grove grew brighter with each turn of the cane.

When the mixture began to glow with a steady golden light, Mia placed the candy cane in the center of the altar and stepped back. "What now?" she asked, her voice trembling.

Nan pointed to the Codex. "Read the incantation. Let the words guide you."

Mia's eyes scanned the golden script, and she began to speak:

"By the sweetness of joy and the warmth of cheer,
Rekindle the magic we hold dear.
Let love and wonder fill the air,

And banish all shadows of despair.
With heart and hope, we make this plea:
Restore the glow for all to see."

As Mia's voice rang through the grove, the mixture on the altar began to pulse with light. A soft hum filled the air, growing louder and more harmonious. The candy cane in the center of the altar lifted into the air, spinning slowly as it absorbed the glowing paste. Rays of light shot outward, illuminating the entire grove and painting the sky with a kaleidoscope of colors.

The peppermint trees shuddered, their stripes glowing brighter, and the snow sparkled as if infused with starlight. The candy cane spun faster and faster until, with a burst of light, it shattered into a thousand smaller candy canes that rained down like snowflakes.

Each candy cane landed softly on the ground, radiating joy and warmth. The grove seemed to sigh with relief, its magic restored.

Nan stepped forward, her eyes shining with pride. "You've done it, Mia. The candy canes are re-enchanted, and the Yuletide Glow is stronger than ever."

Mia felt a swell of pride, but before she could speak, the grove itself seemed to respond. The trees bent slightly, as if bowing, and a soft, melodic voice echoed through the air:

"A new Keeper has risen, one pure of heart.
Guide us well, and let the magic never part."

Nan smiled and placed a hand on Mia's shoulder. "The grove has chosen you, Mia. You are now the Keeper of Conjurations, responsible for protecting the magic of Christmas and ensuring its joy endures for generations."

Mia's eyes widened. "Me? But I—"

"You've proven yourself," Nan said gently. "This is your destiny."

Toby grinned, clapping her on the back. "Guess that makes me the Keeper's assistant, huh?"

"And I'll be here to keep you on your toes," Cane added with a wink.

As the grove settled into a peaceful glow, Mia felt a sense of purpose unlike anything she had ever known. The journey had been daunting, but it had shown her the strength she didn't know she possessed—and the magic she was capable of creating.

With the candy canes' enchantment restored and Christmas magic secured, Mia knew her adventures were far from over. The role of Keeper of Conjurations promised challenges and discoveries she couldn't yet imagine. But for now, she stood in the heart of the Peppermint Grove, surrounded by her friends and the radiant glow of Christmas magic, ready to embrace whatever came next.

Appendix A: The Lore of Candy Cane Magic

The magic of candy canes is as ancient as the Yuletide Glow itself, woven into the very fabric of Christmas. While most see these striped confections as simple holiday treats, they are, in truth, powerful artifacts crafted through the ingenuity and dedication of the **Holiday Magicians**, an ancient order of conjurers tasked with preserving the spirit of Christmas. This appendix delves into the origins of candy cane enchantments, their creators, the critical role they play in spreading joy, and the unique properties of the Peppermint Grove where they are born.

The Origins of Candy Cane Magic

The story of candy cane magic begins centuries ago, during the First Yule. At that time, the Yuletide Glow, a mystical force that embodies joy, generosity, and hope, was at risk of fading due to rising bitterness and despair in the world. The Holiday Magicians, led by the legendary **Auroria Frostwillow**, recognized that this glow needed a physical medium to anchor it and keep it from dissipating.

Auroria, inspired by the purity of snow and the sweetness of candy, developed the first enchanted candy canes. These early prototypes were simple in appearance but brimming with magic. Their iconic red and white stripes symbolized the dual powers of **love (red)** and **purity (white)**, while their peppermint flavor was chosen for its calming and restorative properties. The crook at the top of the candy cane was a deliberate nod to the shepherd's staff, a symbol of guidance and protection, reminding all who held it of their duty to spread kindness.

The Holiday Magicians: Keepers of the Enchantment

The Holiday Magicians were a secretive order of highly skilled conjurers and alchemists who dedicated their lives to safeguarding Christmas magic. Members included individuals from all walks of life, united by their deep connection to the Yuletide Glow.

Notable Figures:

- **Auroria Frostwillow:** The visionary who created the first candy cane enchantments and established the rituals still used today.
- **Elder Canehart:** A meticulous alchemist who perfected the recipe for Stardust Sugar and its binding properties.
- **Sylveris Duskpine:** The guardian of the Frosted Forest, who ensured the sustainability of its magical ecosystem for ingredient harvesting.

Each magician played a vital role in maintaining the enchantments. Over time, the candy canes became essential tools in spreading holiday cheer, their magic influencing everything from familial bonds to global goodwill.

The Enchantment Process

Candy cane enchantments are a delicate blend of alchemy, spellcraft, and heartfelt intention. The process involves gathering rare ingredients, each imbued with unique properties, and combining them through rituals that channel the Yuletide Glow. The final step involves infusing the candy cane with magical symbols that lock in its power.

Magical Symbols:

- **The Swirl of Serenity:** A spiral symbol representing the continuous flow of joy and calm. This is inscribed on the candy cane's core to stabilize its energy.
- **The Spark of Cheer:** A star-like glyph added to amplify the candy cane's ability to spread happiness.
- **The Rune of Binding:** A looping symbol that binds the magical properties of the ingredients to the candy cane, ensuring its longevity.

Below is a diagram of the symbols used in the enchantment process:

[Diagram]

1. The Swirl of Serenity: A spiral with gentle, outward-turning loops.

2. The Spark of Cheer: A five-pointed star surrounded by tiny dots of light.

3. The Rune of Binding: An infinity-shaped loop with a small heart at the center.

The Role of Candy Canes in Maintaining Christmas Joy

Candy canes are more than magical objects; they are conduits of Christmas spirit, designed to restore faith, heal broken relationships, and inspire acts of kindness. Their magic works subtly, weaving its influence into everyday moments:

- **Protection:** Placed in homes, candy canes create a barrier against negativity, safeguarding holiday joy.
- **Inspiration:** Those who consume or hold an enchanted candy cane often find themselves filled with generosity and warmth.
- **Unity:** Candy canes strengthen bonds between people, reminding them of the importance of togetherness during the holiday season.

The Peppermint Grove: Birthplace of Enchantment

The Peppermint Grove is the sacred birthplace of all enchanted candy canes. Located in an ever-winter realm hidden from the mortal world, the grove is a marvel of natural and magical beauty. Its unique properties make it the ideal location for candy cane creation.

Unique Properties of the Grove:

- **Self-Sustaining Ecosystem:** The grove's peppermint trees produce endless supplies of pure peppermint sap, which is critical for the candy canes' flavor and magical resonance.
- **Time Flux:** Time flows differently in the grove, allowing conjurers to work without the constraints of ordinary days and nights.
- **Enhanced Magic:** The very soil of the grove is infused with residual Yuletide Glow, amplifying the effectiveness of all rituals performed within its bounds.

The grove is protected by powerful enchantments and guardians such as the **Sugar Sprites** and **Aurora Wards**, ensuring that only those with pure intentions can enter.

The Legacy of Candy Cane Magic

Through the ages, candy canes have become symbols of hope and resilience. They remind the world that even in the darkest times, sweetness and joy can prevail. The rituals of enchantment continue to evolve, passed down through generations of Keepers of Conjurations, like Mia, ensuring the magic remains alive.

As long as there are candy canes in the world, the Yuletide Glow will burn bright, and the spirit of Christmas will endure.

This appendix honors the history and craftsmanship behind one of the season's most beloved traditions, revealing the depth of magic behind its simple sweetness. For those who hold a candy cane this season, know that you are holding a piece of ancient enchantment, a testament to the enduring power of love, joy, and holiday cheer.

Appendix B: Magical Ingredients and Creatures

This appendix serves as a comprehensive guide to the magical ingredients and fantastical beings encountered throughout the journey to save the Yuletide Glow. From the shimmering Stardust Sugar to the enigmatic Sugar Sprites, each entity plays a vital role in the world of Christmas magic. Learn about their origins, properties, and how to interact with these wonders responsibly.

Magical Ingredients

1. Stardust Sugar

- **Description:** Stardust Sugar is a luminous, sand-like substance that glows with the light of distant stars. Found exclusively on the Celestial Confectionery, it is both delicate and immensely powerful. Its grains are infused with the essence of joy and wonder, making it a critical ingredient in candy cane enchantments.
- **Properties:**
    - Emits a soft golden glow, symbolizing hope.
    - Amplifies the magic of any enchantment it is added to.
    - Dissolves into a warm, sweet mist when used in rituals.
- **Harvesting Tips:** Stardust Sugar can only be collected from the **Sands of Radiance**, a glowing dune hidden within the Celestial Confectionery's labyrinth. Collect it using enchanted glass jars to prevent its light from fading.

2. Frozen Mint Crystals

- **Description:** These radiant blue crystals form naturally in the Frosted Vale, suspended in icicles hanging from the Vale's tallest trees. Their minty aroma is invigorating, and their magical properties are unmatched in their ability to restore and fortify enchantments.
- **Properties:**
  - Absorbs and reflects light, creating a calming aura.
  - Strengthens spells that involve protection or healing.
  - Melts into a minty, rejuvenating elixir when exposed to heat.
- **Guardians:** Frozen Mint Crystals are fiercely protected by the **Ice Elves**, who ensure their harvesting does not disrupt the forest's balance.
- **Harvesting Tips:** Approach with respect and seek permission from the Ice Elves. The crystals must be chipped gently with a silver tool to retain their potency.

3. Aurora Honey

- **Description:** Collected from the **Northern Lights Bees**, this shimmering honey glows with the iridescent hues of the Aurora Borealis. It is incredibly rare and prized for its ability to infuse spells with harmony and unity.
- **Properties:**
    - Emits a soothing, melodic hum when warmed.
    - Enhances emotional resonance in enchantments.
    - Highly versatile in alchemical applications.
- **Harvesting Tips:** To collect Aurora Honey, follow the bees' migration to their hives under the Northern Lights. Approach the hives with reverence, as the bees are sensitive to negative emotions. Use enchanted gloves to avoid harming the hive.

4. Gingerroot Essence

- **Description:** Found deep within the labyrinthine caves of the Gingerbread Mountains, this essence is distilled from magical ginger roots that grow only in enchanted soil. Its spicy aroma is both invigorating and grounding.
- **Properties:**
    - Adds stability to complex enchantments.
    - Generates warmth and resilience in protective spells.
    - Energizes the user when consumed.
- **Harvesting Tips:** The roots must be unearthed carefully under moonlight, as their potency diminishes in sunlight. Use a copper blade for precise extraction.

5. Cinnamon Spark

- **Description:** This fiery spice is mined from the heart of the **Ember Pines**, ancient trees that burn eternally without being consumed. The sparks are gathered from the glowing embers scattered at their roots.
- **Properties:**
    - Adds energy and passion to spells.
    - Ignites warmth in environments filled with cold or despair.
    - Functions as a catalyst in transformational magic.
- **Harvesting Tips:** Wear heat-resistant gloves when collecting sparks. Recite a calming charm to prevent the embers from flaring unpredictably.

Magical Creatures

1. Sugar Sprites

- **Description:** These playful, winged creatures are guardians of the Stardust Sugar. They are no larger than teacups, with translucent wings that shimmer like spun sugar and a glow that reflects their emotions.
- **Behavior:** Mischievous but not malevolent, Sugar Sprites enjoy riddles and games. They are wary of strangers but can be won over with cleverness and kindness.
- **Tips for Interaction:**
  - Always answer their riddles honestly. Lying will offend them.
  - Bring a small offering, such as a piece of festive candy, to show goodwill.

2. Ice Elves

- **Description:** Slender, blue-skinned beings with sharp, crystalline features, Ice Elves are the protectors of the Frosted Vale. They are deeply connected to the frozen landscape and its magic.
- **Behavior:** Stoic and cautious, Ice Elves value honor and integrity. They are slow to trust but fiercely loyal once a bond is formed.
- **Tips for Interaction:**
  - Show respect and humility. Bowing upon meeting them is customary.
  - Be prepared to prove your intentions through tests of character, such as the **Reflection of Truth.**

3. The Sourling

- **Description:** A dark, twisted creature born from bitterness and despair, the Sourling feeds on lost holiday cheer. Its grotesque form shifts constantly, with gnarled limbs and glowing, venomous eyes.
- **Behavior:** The Sourling is hostile and destructive, but it is not inherently evil. Its bitterness stems from pain and forgotten joy.
- **Tips for Interaction:**
    - Avoid fear and anger, as these emotions empower it.
    - Use symbols of love and kindness to weaken its influence.
    - Transforming the Sourling requires patience, compassion, and a strong heart.

Conclusion

These magical ingredients and creatures are more than fantastical elements of Christmas—they are integral to the balance and preservation of the Yuletide Glow. Respecting their origins, understanding their roles, and interacting with them responsibly ensures that their magic will continue to inspire wonder and joy for generations to come.

<u>Message from the Author:</u>

I hope you enjoyed this book, I love astrology and knew there was not a book such as this out on the shelf. I love metaphysical items as well. Please check out my other books:

-Life of Government Benefits

-My life of Hell

-My life with Hydrocephalus

-Red Sky

-World Domination:Woman's rule

-World Domination:Woman's Rule 2: The War

-Life and Banishment of Apophis: book 1

-The Kidney Friendly Diet

-The Ultimate Hemp Cookbook

-Creating a Dispensary(legally)

-Cleanliness throughout life: the importance of showering from childhood to adulthood.

-Strong Roots: The Risks of Overcoddling children

-Hemp Horoscopes: Cosmic Insights and Earthly Healing

- Celestial Hemp Navigating the Zodiac: Through the Green Cosmos

-Astrological Hemp: Aligning The Stars with Earth's Ancient Herb

-The Astrological Guide to Hemp: Stars, Signs, and Sacred Leaves

-Green Growth: Innovative Marketing Strategies for your Hemp Products and Dispensary

-Cosmic Cannabis

-Astrological Munchies

-Henry The Hemp

-Zodiacal Roots: The Astrological Soul Of Hemp

- Green Constellations: Intersection of Hemp and Zodiac

-Hemp in The Houses: An astrological Adventure Through The Cannabis Galaxy

-Galactic Ganja Guide

Heavenly Hemp

Zodiac Leaves

Doctor Who Astrology

Cannastrology

Stellar Satvias and Cosmic Indicas

<u>Celestial Cannabis: A Zodiac Journey</u>

AstroHerbology: The Sky and The Soil: Volume 1

AstroHerbology:Celestial Cannabis:Volume 2

Cosmic Cannabis Cultivation

The Starry Guide to Herbal Harmony: Volume 1

The Starry Guide to Herbal Harmony: Cannabis Universe: Volume 2

Yugioh Astrology: Astrological Guide to Deck, Duels and more

Nightmare Mansion: Echoes of The Abyss

Nightmare Mansion 2: Legacy of Shadows

Nightmare Mansion 3: Shadows of the Forgotten

Nightmare Mansion 4: Echoes of the Damned

The Life and Banishment of Apophis: Book 2

Nightmare Mansion: Halls of Despair

<u>Healing with Herb: Cannabis and Hydrocephalus</u>

<u>Planetary Pot: Aligning with Astrological Herbs: Volume 1</u>

Fast Track to Freedom: 30 Days to Financial Independence Using AI, Assets, and Agile Hustles

<u>Cosmic Hemp Pathways</u>

How to Become Financially Free in 30 Days: 10,000 Paths to Prosperity

Zodiacal Herbage: Astrological Insights: Volume 1

Nightmare Mansion: Whispers in the Walls

The Daleks Invade Atlantis
Henry the hemp and Hydrocephalus

10X The Kidney Friendly Diet
Cannabis Universe: Adult coloring book
Hemp Astrology: The Healing Power of the Stars
Zodiacal Herbage: Astrological Insights: Cannabis Universe: Volume 2
<u>Planetary Pot: Aligning with Astrological Herbs: Cannabis Universes: Volume 2</u>
Doctor Who Meets the Replicators and SG-1: The Ultimate Battle for Survival
Nightmare Mansion: Curse of the Blood Moon
<u>The Celestial Stoner: A Guide to the Zodiac</u>
Cosmic Pleasures: Sex Toy Astrology for Every Sign
Hydrocephalus Astrology: Navigating the Stars and Healing Waters
Lapis and the Mischievous Chocolate Bar

Celestial Positions: Sexual Astrology for Every Sign
Apophis's Shadow Work Journal: : A Journey of Self-Discovery and Healing
Kinky Cosmos: Sexual Kink Astrology for Every Sign
Digital Cosmos: The Astrological Digimon Compendium
Stellar Seeds: The Cosmic Guide to Growing with Astrology
Apophis's Daily Gratitude Journal

Cat Astrology: Feline Mysteries of the Cosmos
The Cosmic Kama Sutra: An Astrological Guide to Sexual Positions
Unleash Your Potential: A Guided Journal Powered by AI Insights
Whispers of the Enchanted Grove

Cosmic Pleasures: An Astrological Guide to Sexual Kinks

369, 12 Manifestation Journal

Whisper of the nocturne journal(blank journal for writing or drawing)

The Boogey Book

Locked In Reflection: A Chastity Journey Through Locktober

Generating Wealth Quickly:

How to Generate $100,000 in 24 Hours

Star Magic: Harness the Power of the Universe

The Flatulence Chronicles: A Fart Journal for Self-Discovery

The Doctor and The Death Moth

Seize the Day: A Personal Seizure Tracking Journal

The Ultimate Boogeyman Safari: A Journey into the Boogie World and Beyond

Whispers of Samhain: 1,000 Spells of Love, Luck, and Lunar Magic: Samhain Spell Book

Apophis's guides:

Witch's Spellbook Crafting Guide for Halloween

<u>Frost & Flame: The Enchanted Yule Grimoire of 1000 Winter Spells</u>

<u>The Ultimate Boogey Goo Guide & Spooky Activities for Halloween Fun</u>

Harmony of the Scales: A Libra's Spellcraft for Balance and Beauty

The Enchanted Advent: 36 Days of Christmas Wonders

Nightmare Mansion: The Labyrinth of Screams

Harvest of Enchantment: 1,000 Spells of Gratitude, Love, and Fortune for Thanksgiving

The Boogey Chronicles: A Journal of Nightly Encounters and Shadowy Secrets

The 12 Days of Financial Freedom: A Step-by-Step Christmas Countdown to Transform Your Finances

Prehistoric Palettes: A Dino Wicca Coloring Journey
The Christmas Wishkeeper Chronicles
The Starlight Sleigh: A Holiday Journey
Elf Secrets: The True Magic of the North Pole
If you want solar for your home go here: https://www.harborsolar.live/apophisenterprises/

Get Some Tarot cards: https://www.makeplayingcards.com/sell/apophis-occult-shop

Get   some   shirts: https://www.bonfire.com/store/apophis-shirt-emporium/

<u>**Instagrams:**</u>
@apophis_enterprises,
@apophisbookemporium,
@apophisscardshop
Twitter: @apophisenterpr1
 Tiktok:@apophisenterprise
Youtube: @sg1fan23477, @FiresideRetreatKingdom
Hive: @sg1fan23477
CheeLee: @SG1fan23477

Podcast: Apophis Chat Zone: https://open.spotify.com/show/
5zXbrCLEV2xzCp8ybrfHsk?si=fb4d4fdbdce44dec

Newsletter: https://apophiss-newsletter-27c897.beehiiv.com/

If you want to support me or see posts of other projects that I have come over to: **buymeacoffee.com/mpetchinskg**
I post there daily several times a day

Get your Dinowicca or Christmas themed digital products, especially Santa Raptor songs and other musics. Here: **https://sg1fan23477.gumroad.com**

Apophis Yuletide Digital has not only digital Christmas items, but it will have all things with Dinowicca as well as other Digital products.